The Boxcar Children

The Boxcar Children
Surprise Island
The Yellow House Mystery
Mystery Ranch
Mike's Mystery
Blue Bay Mystery
The Woodshed Mystery
The Lighthouse Mystery
Mountain Top Mystery
Schoolhouse Mystery
Caboose Mystery
Houseboat Mystery
Snowbound Mystery
Tree House Mystery
Bicycle Mystery
Mystery in the Sand
Mystery Behind the Wall
Bus Station Mystery
Benny Uncovers a Mystery
The Haunted Cabin Mystery
The Deserted Library Mystery
The Animal Shelter Mystery
The Old Motel Mystery
The Mystery of the Hidden Painting
The Amusement Park Mystery
The Mystery of the Mixed-Up Zoo
The Camp-Out Mystery
The Mystery Girl
The Mystery Cruise
The Disappearing Friend Mystery
The Mystery of the Singing Ghost
The Mystery in the Snow
The Pizza Mystery
The Mystery Horse
The Mystery at the Dog Show
The Castle Mystery
The Mystery of the Lost Village
The Mystery on the Ice
The Mystery of the Purple Pool
The Ghost Ship Mystery
The Mystery in Washington, DC
The Canoe Trip Mystery
The Mystery of the Hidden Beach
The Mystery of the Missing Cat
The Mystery at Snowflake Inn
The Mystery on Stage
The Dinosaur Mystery
The Mystery of the Stolen Music
The Mystery at the Ball Park
The Chocolate Sundae Mystery
The Mystery of the Hot Air Balloon
The Mystery Bookstore
The Pilgrim Village Mystery
The Mystery of the Stolen Boxcar
The Mystery in the Cave
The Mystery on the Train
The Mystery at the Fair
The Mystery of the Lost Mine
The Guide Dog Mystery
The Hurricane Mystery
The Pet Shop Mystery
The Mystery of the Secret Message
The Firehouse Mystery
The Mystery in San Francisco
The Niagara Falls Mystery
The Mystery at the Alamo
The Outer Space Mystery
The Soccer Mystery
The Mystery in the Old Attic
The Growling Bear Mystery
The Mystery of the Lake Monster
The Mystery at Peacock Hall
The Windy City Mystery
The Black Pearl Mystery
The Cereal Box Mystery
The Panther Mystery
The Mystery of the Queen's Jewels
The Stolen Sword Mystery
The Basketball Mystery
The Movie Star Mystery
The Mystery of the Pirate's Map
The Ghost Town Mystery
The Mystery of the Black Raven
The Mystery in the Mall

The Boxcar Children Mysteries

The Mystery in New York
The Gymnastics Mystery
The Poison Frog Mystery
The Mystery of the Empty Safe
The Home Run Mystery
The Great Bicycle Race Mystery
The Mystery of the Wild Ponies
The Mystery in the Computer Game
The Honeybee Mystery
The Mystery at the Crooked House
The Hockey Mystery
The Mystery of the Midnight Dog
The Mystery of the Screech Owl
The Summer Camp Mystery
The Copycat Mystery
The Haunted Clock Tower Mystery
The Mystery of the Tiger's Eye
The Disappearing Staircase Mystery
The Mystery on Blizzard Mountain
The Mystery of the Spider's Clue
The Candy Factory Mystery
The Mystery of the Mummy's Curse
The Mystery of the Star Ruby
The Stuffed Bear Mystery
The Mystery of Alligator Swamp
The Mystery at Skeleton Point
The Tattletale Mystery
The Comic Book Mystery
The Great Shark Mystery
The Ice Cream Mystery
The Midnight Mystery
The Mystery in the Fortune Cookie
The Black Widow Spider Mystery
The Radio Mystery
The Mystery of the Runaway Ghost
The Finders Keepers Mystery
The Mystery of the Haunted Boxcar
The Clue in the Corn Maze
The Ghost of the Chattering Bones
The Sword of the Silver Knight
The Game Store Mystery
The Mystery of the Orphan Train
The Vanishing Passenger
The Giant Yo-Yo Mystery
The Creature in Ogopogo Lake
The Rock 'n' Roll Mystery
The Secret of the Mask
The Seattle Puzzle
The Ghost in the First Row
The Box That Watch Found
A Horse Named Dragon
The Great Detective Race
The Ghost at the Drive-In Movie
The Mystery of the Traveling Tomatoes
The Spy Game
The Dog-Gone Mystery
The Vampire Mystery
Superstar Watch
The Spy in the Bleachers
The Amazing Mystery Show
The Pumpkin Head Mystery
The Cupcake Caper
The Clue in the Recycling Bin
Monkey Trouble
The Zombie Project
The Great Turkey Heist
The Garden Thief
The Boardwalk Mystery
The Mystery of the Fallen Treasure
The Return of the Graveyard Ghost
The Mystery of the Stolen Snowboard
The Mystery of the Wild West Bandit
The Mystery of the Grinning Gargoyle
The Mystery of the Soccer Snitch
The Mystery of the Missing Pop Idol
The Mystery of the Stolen Dinosaur Bones
The Mystery at the Calgary Stampede
The Sleepy Hollow Mystery
The Legend of the Irish Castle
The Celebrity Cat Caper
Hidden in the Haunted School
The Election Day Dilemma

THE MYSTERY AT PEACOCK HALL

created by
GERTRUDE CHANDLER WARNER

Illustrated by Charles Tang

Albert Whitman & Company
Chicago, Illinois

ISBN 978-0-8075-5445-6

Printed in the United States of America
10 9 8 7 6 LB 20 19 18 17 16

Illustrated by Charles Tang

For more information about Albert Whitman & Company, visit our website at www.albertwhitman.com.

Contents

CHAPTER 1

"Come at Once!"

From the front seat of the station wagon, Benny Alden traced the large *R* at the top of the letter with his finger.

"What did you say this was again?" he asked his grandfather.

"A monogram," replied Grandfather. "The first letter is a person's last name. Our monogram would be *A* for Alden."

"A monogram is an initial," said Jessie from the backseat. "Initials are the first letters of your name. Your initials are —"

"*B, A*!" Benny finished. At six, he was just

learning to read. His sister Jessie, who was twelve, was teaching him more each day.

Next to Jessie, ten-year-old Violet turned from the window. "When I grow up, I'm going to have thick writing paper with my monogram on it in gold, just like Cousin Althea's."

It had only been a few days ago that the letter from Althea Randolph had arrived. It had a gold monogram on the envelope. Grandfather had opened it right away.

Althea Randolph was a cousin of Grandfather's wife, Celia. In the letter, Althea claimed to be in trouble and needed Grandfather's help.

The Alden children and their grandfather always tried to help people. Once, Henry, Jessie, Violet, and Benny had lived in an old boxcar. Their parents had died, and they were afraid their grandfather was mean. But then he had found them, and the children had learned that James Alden was a kind and loving man.

Grandfather decided immediately that they would go to Virginia, where Althea lived in a house called Peacock Hall. The Aldens packed, took a plane to Richmond, Virginia, then rented a car to drive to the Randolph estate.

Now they were driving past emerald-green pastures with grazing horses. Violet wished she had brought her camera. The chestnut horses would make a great picture. But they had left in such a hurry, she forgot to pack it.

"I wonder what kind of trouble Cousin Althea is in," she said.

Grandfather shook his head. "She didn't say in her letter. She just asked for us to come at once. We've been on this road quite a while. I'm not sure this is the right way."

Benny pointed. "Look! There's a lady selling stuff. Let's stop and ask her."

"Good idea." Grandfather pulled the station wagon off the road.

The kids piled out, glad to stretch after the long ride.

A woman in her late twenties was arranging jars of small plants on a rough wooden counter. Wreaths of grapevine and dried flowers hung from the front of the handmade stall. A boy about Violet's age watered buckets of flowers.

"Can I help you?" the woman said. Jessie thought she was pretty, with strawberry-blond hair and eyes so blue they were nearly purple.

"We're looking for a house called Peacock Hall," said Grandfather. "Do you know if this is the right road?"

"Yes, it is," the woman replied in a soft Virginia drawl. "Keep going about a mile, to the old stone wall. The driveway is on the right. There's a sign, but it's grown over with trees."

"Thank you," Grandfather said.

Benny was interested in the weird-smelling plants on the counter.

"Those are herbs," the woman told him.

Benny wrinkled his nose. "What are herbs?"

"Plants used in cooking. And people like them just because they smell nice, too." The woman pulled off a leaf and crushed it between her fingers. "What's that smell like?"

Benny sniffed. "Lemon!"

"Very good! The plant is called lemon balm."

Jessie chose a bunch of wildflowers. "Do you think Cousin Althea would like these?" she asked.

"They are pretty. By the way, I'm Heather Olsen and this is my son, David. Hope to see you again."

"Do you live around here?" Grandfather asked Heather as he paid for the purchase.

"Yeah, we live —" David began.

But Heather interrupted loudly, "David! Don't drown the daffodils!"

He glanced down at the watering can, suddenly silent.

"Thanks very much for your help," said Henry, who was fourteen.

They all got back in the station wagon.

Violet watched David as they drove off. The boy didn't look up. "David seems kind of strange."

"Maybe he's just shy," Jessie said, burying

her nose in the bouquet of spring blooms.

But Violet didn't think so. She thought David was about to say something and his mother stopped him. But she forgot about Heather and David as Grandfather turned the car onto a pitted asphalt lane.

"Boy," said Benny. "This is the longest driveway."

"It *is* long," Grandfather agreed, as the car bounced over a pothole. "Althea could use a load of gravel in these holes. And those bushes need to be cut back."

Locust trees and honeysuckle vines grew densely along each side. The thick shrubbery gave Jessie the creeps. If the driveway was this bad, what would the house be like?

Suddenly the trees gave way to a wide, sloping lawn. The land looped around a crumbling goldfish pond. A large stone fish balanced on its tail in the center of the empty pool.

Jessie gasped when she saw the house. Three stories of pinkish red brick soared above a half-moon porch. Massive white pillars supported the porch roof. A brick-paved walk, bordered by red and yellow tulips, led to the steps.

"Wow!" Benny exclaimed. "What a big house!"

Grandfather parked the car. "Yes, Peacock Hall is quite impressive. But the porch needs painting and the flower beds are full of weeds. Why has Althea let the place get so run-down?"

Everyone climbed out. Henry unloaded the luggage and they each took a bag up the steps.

Grandfather rang the bell. After a short pause, the heavy oak door swung inward.

"James!" said the old woman who stood there. "I'm so glad you're here! And you brought your grandchildren!"

"Hello, Althea," said Grandfather, putting out his hand. "Yes, these are my grandchildren. This is Henry, Jessie, Violet, and Benny."

"Welcome," Althea Randolph greeted them. "Please come in! You must be exhausted after that trip."

She led them down a long hall and into

a high-ceilinged room with peach-colored walls. Portraits of stern-looking men and women glared down at the visitors.

"Sit down," Althea offered. "I've made some lemonade."

While Althea poured drinks, Jessie studied her cousin. She was older than Grandfather. Snow-white curls framed a face that was still pretty. Althea wore a lace-collared print dress with a silver pin.

Grandfather accepted his glass with a nod of thanks. "Althea, do you live here alone? I know your husband passed away some years ago."

"Yes," Althea replied. "Grayson died eight years ago. We had no children, you know. Old Tate lives on the grounds. He's the gardener, but he doesn't do much these days."

"How old is this house?" Henry asked, looking at the iron implements hanging from the fireplace.

Althea brightened. "Peacock Hall is very old. It was originally built in 1814 by my husband's ancestor, Zachary Randolph. Zachary was friends with Thomas Jefferson. Did you know that Monticello, Jefferson's estate, is nearby?"

Henry nodded. "Thomas Jefferson was the third president."

Violet felt like she was living in a history lesson. "How did the house get its name?"

"Zachary brought a pair of peacocks with him from England," Althea replied. "Well, a peacock and a peahen, as the female bird is called. Anyway, it's family tradition that there are always peacocks on the lawn."

Benny's eyes grew bright. "Where are the peacocks now?" He'd seen pictures of the colorful birds.

"You'll see them," Althea said. Then she added soberly, "Though I don't know how long the tradition will last."

Grandfather said, "Your letter sounded urgent."

Althea's blue eyes clouded. "Oh, James, I'm in such terrible trouble! I owe some money in back taxes on this place. If I don't pay by Friday, I'll be evicted and Peacock Hall will be auctioned!"

"Can they do that?" asked Jessie. She couldn't believe Althea could be thrown out of her own house.

"Yes, they can," said Grandfather. "Althea, did Grayson leave you his estate when he died?"

She dabbed a tissue at her eyes. "Yes, he left me the house and what was in our bank account. We never had much money. Peacock Hall is expensive to run. Something is always breaking, like the furnace or the plumbing. Grayson told me he never wanted Peacock Hall to leave the Randolph family. The Randolphs built this house and kept it even during difficult times."

Grandfather frowned. "You and Grayson didn't have children. Are there any other Randolphs who might buy it?"

"Grayson had some distant cousins," Althea replied. "But they're scattered all over the country. They don't want to be burdened with a white elephant in Virginia."

Benny leaned forward. "White elephant? Where?" He loved elephants. When he grew up, he planned to own one.

Althea laughed. "It's an expression, Benny, dear. A white elephant is a big place nobody wants."

Jessie rubbed her hand over the worn chair cushion. She could see why Peacock Hall might be hard to sell. People today wanted new houses.

Footsteps rang across the foyer. Henry, who was sitting closest to the doorway, saw a red-faced young man rush into the room.

"Aunt Althea!" the man thundered. "If you're going behind my back and selling to a real estate agent —"

"Roscoe Janney!" Althea chided. "Where are your manners? This gentleman is my cousin Celia's husband, James Alden. And these are his grandchildren. They've come to visit me."

"Oh." Roscoe looked embarrassed. "Aunt Althea, have you considered my offer — will you sell Peacock Hall? You could get a cozy little apartment in Charlottesville."

Althea drew herself up. "First of all, Roscoe, your paltry offer is an insult. Peacock Hall is worth twice that price. And second, let me remind you that although you *are* my great-nephew, you are *not* a Randolph."

Roscoe's beady eyes narrowed. "By Friday you're going to wish you had snapped up my offer. Only by then it'll be too late!" He turned on his heel and left, slamming the front door behind him.

"I apologize for my great-nephew's behavior," Althea said to Grandfather. "He's right about one thing, though. By Friday I'll have to leave."

"Have you had any other offers?" Grandfather asked.

"One. A woman named Marlene Sanders came by a month ago. She offered me a fair price, but the development firm she represents wants to tear the house down and put up a golf course!" Althea seemed ready to cry. "If I sell, what will happen to old Tate? I hate to go against my husband's wish. I promised him I'd only sell this house to a member of the Randolph family."

Grandfather patted Althea's hand. "It'll be all right. But we can't fix your problem tonight. Tomorrow is Monday. I'll go downtown and check the county records."

The older woman looked relieved. "The taxes are due Friday at five o'clock. I'd be so grateful if you stayed until then."

Grandfather pushed himself to his feet. "My grandchildren are very helpful as well. They've solved a number of mystery cases."

"You don't say!" Althea smiled. "Maybe you children will find the secret of Peacock Hall."

Benny, who was nodding off, became alert. "Mystery? There's a mystery here? Tell us about it!"

Grandfather laughed. "Not tonight. We've had a long day and it's bedtime."

"I'll show you to your rooms," Althea led them up a wide flight of stairs and down a hallway. "I'm afraid I don't use these rooms anymore, so you'll have to make up your own beds. Linens are in this closet."

Benny and Henry chose a blue-painted room overlooking the empty fish pond. The girls picked a room across the hall with rose-patterned wallpaper.

Violet sneezed when she opened the linen closet. "Whew! Nobody's used these sheets in ages." She took out sheets and pillowcases for four twin beds. Handing two sets to her brothers, she said good night.

In their room, Jessie began making up their beds. "This house needs a good cleaning!"

Violet yawned hugely. "Please. I'm too tired to think about cleaning tonight."

They climbed into bed and Jessie switched off the old-fashioned lamp on the nightstand.

Scritch-scritch.

"What's that?" Violet asked.

Jessie was nearly asleep. "What's what?"

"That scratching sound. Hear it?" Violet sat up.

"Maybe it's a tree branch outside," Jessie said drowsily.

But Violet had to see. She slid out of bed and padded over to the window.

A face peered back at her!

CHAPTER 2

Mr. Jefferson's House

Violet shouted, "Somebody's out there!"

Jessie threw back the covers and dashed to the window. "I don't see anyone. Are you sure?"

"Positive!" Violet thrust back the rose-bud-sprigged curtains. A soft mist had drifted in from the hills. It was hard to see clearly. Still, Violet knew she had seen a face.

Feet pounded down the hall. The others had heard Violet's cry. Grandfather burst

into the room, Henry and Benny at his heels.

"What is it?" Grandfather said.

"I saw someone looking in the window!" Violet answered.

Althea Randolph appeared wearing an old velvet bathrobe. "You must have been dreaming, child. We're two stories up."

Grandfather looked through the window. "If Violet says she saw someone out here, she did. Henry, you're still dressed. Come with me. We'll look outside."

Benny held out his flashlight. It was new and he never went anywhere without it. "Take this, Grandfather."

"Thanks, Benny. Henry and I will be back in a minute."

Everyone went downstairs to wait in the living room.

Violet was still shaking. She couldn't tell if the face had belonged to a man or a woman. But she knew she hadn't been dreaming.

Henry came back in, followed by Grandfather, who gave Benny his flashlight.

"Did you find anything?" Benny asked.

"Marks in the dirt under the second-story window," Henry reported. "Probably from a ladder. Violet was right — someone was there."

Althea put a hand to her cheek. "Oh, my! In all my years here, I can't recall ever having a burglar."

"The person is gone now," Grandfather assured her.

They all went back to bed. Violet didn't think she could fall asleep after so much excitement. She closed her eyes, trying to picture the face at the window.

When she opened them again, birds were singing and spring sunshine filled the room.

Jessie was already up and dressed. She swiped a finger across the dusty dresser. "We have to clean this room!"

Violet groaned, pulling on jeans and a purple T-shirt. "Not before breakfast!"

Jessie was worried. If Althea didn't have any money to pay her taxes, how could she feed five extra people?

She was surprised to walk into the dining room and see the oblong mahogany table set with beautiful china. Althea came in carrying a silver tray loaded with a platter of crisp bacon and fried eggs, a crystal dish of honey, and a basket heaped with homemade biscuits.

"Let me help," Jessie offered. "I love your dishes."

"They've been in my husband's family for many years."

As Jessie placed silver knives and forks around the table, she asked, "This house is important to you, isn't it?"

"I've lived my whole life here, it seems. I can't imagine living anywhere else." Althea left and came back with Grandfather's wildflowers in a tall vase.

Benny skidded into the room. "Oh, boy! Food!"

Jessie laughed. Her little brother wasn't interested in pretty dishes or flowers, only the next meal.

At breakfast, Grandfather announced he

was going into town to go through the county records.

"I want to make sure that tax bill is accurate," he said, draining his coffee cup.

When he left, the children went outside to check where the prowler had been.

Henry showed them several dents in the soft earth near the foundation. "Whoever Violet saw used a ladder to look into the second-story window."

"But why?" asked Violet.

Henry shrugged. "Maybe to scare us."

"Who knows we're here?" Jessie pulled her hair off her neck. The day was warming up fast.

"Nobody, except that great-nephew," Henry replied. "And I don't know why he'd try to scare us."

Benny was staring up at the first-floor window just above his head. "Look!" he said, pointing to something blue caught on the sandstone ledge.

Since he was the tallest, Henry reached up and plucked the scrap of fabric free.

"That's denim," Jessie said. "The material jeans are made out of." She compared the scrap to Violet's jeans.

"A clue," Henry said. "Nice work, Benny. Now we know the prowler is wearing ripped jeans."

"I knew we'd find a mystery here," Violet said.

"Two mysteries," Benny corrected.

"What's the other one?" Jessie wanted to know.

"The secret in this house," Benny reminded them. "Cousin Althea was going to tell us about it, but we had to go to bed. Let's ask her now!"

He ran ahead, leaping up on the front porch and through the wide front door.

Jessie called after him. "Save your energy, Benny! We have some serious housework to do." She looked at Henry and Violet. "You don't mind, do you? I feel sorry for Althea. The house is so big."

"I like old houses," Henry replied. "And this one is neat."

Althea was delighted with Jessie's plan.

She gave them mops, brooms, and cleaning supplies.

But before Benny lifted a dust rag, he had to know about the secret. "You said you'd tell us."

"Oh, that!" said Althea. "It's just a silly story, passed from one generation to the next. Grayson told me there's something in Peacock Hall that's priceless."

"What is it?" asked Violet. She was curious, too.

"I have no idea," their hostess replied. "Grayson didn't know, either. It's truly a secret!"

"It must be a hidden treasure," Benny declared. "We'll find it for you!"

Althea laughed. "If anybody can, I believe you will, Benny Alden! You remind me of Celia when we were growing up. She was so full of life, just like you."

Benny flushed. "We haven't seen the peacocks yet. Where are they?"

"They wander the grounds," Althea told him. "Don't worry. You'll know when they're around," she added with a grin.

The kids started on the top floor. Jessie had never seen so many rooms.

Althea followed them slowly up the steep stairs. "Don't feel you have to scrub every room spotless. I want you to have fun. This afternoon I'll take you to Monticello. I work there two days a week."

With the promise of a treat, the children set to work. Dust vanished from dressers and lamps; windows shone. Soon it was lunchtime. After eating Virginia ham sandwiches, chips, and lemonade, they set off in Althea's ancient car to Monticello.

As they drove down the road, Althea told them a little about Thomas Jefferson.

"As Henry said last night, Jefferson was our third president," Althea said. "He was a great statesman. Jefferson was governor of Virginia. He wrote most of the Declaration of Independence. He was the minister to France, the secretary of state, and the vice president."

"Whew!" Benny remarked. "He was a busy man!"

Althea laughed. "Yes, he was! Besides all

that, Jefferson founded the University of Virginia, built a great mansion, gardened, read, and wrote all his life."

Violet noted the signs they were passing. "What does 'Monticello' mean?"

"It's Italian for 'little mountain.' " Althea turned onto another road that led up and up. "Back when Jefferson was alive, people had to walk up this mountain. It didn't seem so little then! But they agreed it was worth the hike."

Like a jewel, Jefferson's mansion glowed against the velvety lawn. The white dome reflected the sunshine.

Althea parked the car and everyone got out.

Henry gave a low whistle. "Look at that line! I never knew so many people wanted to see this house."

"It's like this every single day," Althea said, waving to the ticket-taker. "But I have a special pass."

They breezed by groups of tourists and into the entrance hall. Althea stopped to tell them more.

"I won't drown you in history," she promised, "but you should know Mr. Jefferson started working on this house when he was twenty-six. He worked on it for forty years. Monticello tells the story of his life better than any biography."

The children gazed around the large, airy room.

"Jefferson was interested in everything," Althea told them. "This entrance hall used to be a sort of museum. Visitors who came saw a fossilized mastodon jawbone, a model of a great pyramid, a buffalo-hide map, and other curiosities. But many of those things are put away now."

Benny was disappointed. The elk antlers were neat, but he really wanted to see a fossil jawbone.

"Let's go into the east portico," Althea said, leading them into the next room. "See the compass on the ceiling? It connects with the weather vane on the roof. Jefferson wanted to know the direction of the wind without having to go outside and look at the weather vane."

"What's that?" Jessie asked, pointing to a strange contraption by the door.

"It's a clock," Althea said. "Jefferson designed it, along with many other inventions we'll see."

Henry examined the cannonball weights on either side of the door. "This is a weird clock."

"Actually, it's very clever." Althea indicated words on the walls. "The cannonballs are attached to those wires. As the weights descend, they pass the days of the week marked on the wall. Not only does the clock tell time, it tells you what day it is!"

Benny peered into a hole cut into the floor where the weights disappeared. "What day is down there?"

Althea laughed. "Okay, so Jefferson wasn't perfect. He made a slight mistake and forgot Saturday."

Jefferson's inventions were all over the house. In the library was a folding table that turned into steps used to reach the top bookcase shelves. Thomas Jefferson wrote so many letters, he invented a device that allowed him to make two copies at the same time.

"I could use that," Violet commented. "Then I wouldn't have to write so many thank-you notes for birthday presents!"

Each of the children had a favorite invention. Henry liked the chaise lounge with candlesticks fitted into the arms and a revolving writing desk.

Jessie thought the music stand was neat. Five racks held sheet music for five musicians and folded into a small box for easy transporting.

Violet decided the bedrooms were the best. Built into cozy alcoves, the beds had overhead storage spaces and porthole windows high above. One bed sported a revolving coat rack at one end that could be turned with a stick.

"You could pick out your clothes without getting up!" she remarked.

But Benny hadn't yet seen the invention that he would like best of all.

CHAPTER 3

A Pair of Ripped Jeans

Althea led them into the dining room just as a tour group was leaving.

"We'll have this room to ourselves until the next group comes," she said.

Benny glanced around. Dining rooms were only interesting when there was food on the table.

"Mr. Jefferson was an intensely private man," Althea was saying. "He wanted his guests to speak freely without servants hanging around. As you may know, Jefferson unfortunately kept many slaves. They carried food from the kitchen through an underground passageway, up a small staircase, and into this room."

Now Benny was fascinated. "Can we see the tunnel?" he asked eagerly.

"I'm sorry, we can't. But," Althea added, "we *can* see this." She walked over to the ornately carved fireplace. "Sometimes the servants would put food on a special elevator in the cellar below. By using pulleys, meals were sent up here."

She pulled open a panel on the side of the fireplace. Inside was a narrow compartment with boxes to hold trays and bottles.

"A dumbwaiter!" Henry exclaimed.

"Wow!" Benny said. "If I had one at home, Mrs. McGregor could send me cookies and milk anytime I wanted!"

Jessie laughed. "Mrs. McGregor is our housekeeper," she explained to Althea.

Althea showed the children a matching secret panel on the other side of the fireplace, then said they ought to go.

"I think Benny is tired," she observed.

"Can we come back to Monticello?"

asked Jessie. "I'd like to see the gardens."

"Absolutely!" Althea said. "I work in the Jefferson Center for Historic Plants tomorrow. You can come with me."

"Did Thomas Jefferson have peacocks?" Benny asked.

Althea shook her head. "But he had a pet mockingbird. When Jefferson lived in the White House, he tamed a mockingbird. The bird sat on his shoulder and chirped in his ear."

Violet was charmed by the story. Jefferson seemed more like a person.

Back at Peacock Hall, the children walked around outside. Daffodils bloomed around the empty goldfish pond, but fall leaves still lay heaped under the pecan trees.

"I thought a gardener lived here," Jessie commented.

Henry nodded. "Tate, Althea called him."

"He doesn't seem to do very much."

Suddenly a loud, eerie sound shattered the stillness.

Jessie got goose bumps. "What was *that*?"

Henry laughed. "I think it's the master of Peacock Hall. He wants to make sure we notice him."

Sure enough, the male peacock strutted around the side of a small brick outbuilding. His folded train swept behind him.

"Oh, boy!" Benny cried. "He's big!"

The children waited, hoping the bird would display his tail. The peahen appeared, too, in her less flashy plumage.

Giving his call again, the peacock lifted his train in a dazzling show of color. He turned in a slow circle.

"He's so beautiful!" breathed Violet. "I wish I had my camera."

"Maybe Cousin Althea has some paper and pens. You can draw him," Jessie suggested.

Benny admired the sapphire "eyes" in the tail feathers. "I'd sure like to have one of those feathers," he said.

"Birds lose their feathers all the time," Henry told him. "You and Watch are always finding blue jay feathers in the grass back home."

"I bet Watch would bark if he saw this big bird," Benny said. He missed his dog, but knew Mrs. McGregor was taking good care of him.

"Henry's right," said Jessie. "Let's see if we can find any feathers."

They walked around the small brick building. In the back was an enclosure made of chicken wire.

Inside the pen were pans of water and cracked corn, and a wooden shelter like a doghouse. But no sapphire-tipped plumes.

"We'll be here all week," Violet assured her little brother. "Maybe we'll find a peacock feather later."

But Benny was staring at something beyond the peacock pen. "Look!" he cried.

Violet turned her head, wondering what was so exciting about a clothesline. T-shirts and jeans hung from a line that was stretched from the small building to a locust tree.

Next to him, Jessie gasped. "Benny, you have sharp eyes!"

"It's just a bunch of laundry—" Henry began. Then he saw it, too. The pair of jeans on the end had a hole in one knee.

"Those jeans!" Violet declared. "I bet the scrap of denim we found this morning matches the hole in those jeans. Henry, do you have it?"

Henry tugged the scrap from his pocket. "Right here. All we have to do is —"

Just then a man came around the corner. He had white hair that stood up in spikes and wore baggy jeans and a plaid flannel shirt. His face was scarlet with anger.

"What do you kids think you're doing?" the man growled.

"Nothing, sir," Henry said politely. "We were just walking around."

The man came up to him. Jessie noted he wasn't much bigger than Henry. He also seemed a lot older than Grandfather. What was he so mad about?

"We're the Aldens," she said, introducing the others. "We're visiting Cousin Althea. You must be Mr. Tate."

The man raised a white eyebrow. "You're with Mr. Alden? Mrs. Randolph said she'd asked him to come."

"That's right," Henry said. "Cousin Althea wrote to our grandfather for help."

"She's a fine lady," the old man remarked. "I hope your granddaddy can get her out of this fix she's in."

"He'll do his best," Violet put in. "Are you the gardener, Mr. Tate?"

He nodded. "Yes, I'm the gardener. I've worked here for fifty years. My daddy was the gardener before me. And my name is just plain Tate."

"Is this your house?" Benny asked, glancing at the brick outbuilding. "We have a little house, too. Not the one we live in now. But we can play in our old house."

Tate looked confused.

Jessie explained, "Benny means we once lived in a boxcar. That was before Grandfather found us. He brought our boxcar to his house and we use it for a sort of clubhouse."

Benny asked Tate again, "Do you live in this house?"

"It's the smokehouse," Tate said, somewhat gruffly. "In the old days, meat was hung in this building to cure. But it's no place for children to fool around. Go on back to the main house, you hear?"

Shocked at the old man's sudden unfriendliness, the Aldens turned and headed toward Peacock Hall.

"What's wrong with *him*?" Violet said.

"I guess he's funny about his place," Henry said with a shrug. "It must be his house. Nobody else lives here but Althea, and she wouldn't hang her laundry way out here."

"She wouldn't wear jeans and T-shirts, either," Jessie added. "But Tate does. Those must be his clothes hanging on that line. And I still think the piece of material we found came from that pair of jeans."

Violet stopped. "Do you think Tate climbed the ladder up to our window last night? Why would he do that?"

Jessie didn't have an answer.

There were many mysteries at Peacock Hall. Would they solve any of them by Friday?

CHAPTER 4

A Whispered Warning

"You heard Grandfather last night," Henry said as they cleared the breakfast dishes the next morning. "Cousin Althea needs nine thousand dollars by Friday. That's three days from now."

The night before, Grandfather brought back groceries along with his grim news. The tax bill was indeed correct. But he would try to get Althea an extension, more time to pay. "Nine thousand dollars!" Benny exclaimed. "That's more than I have in my piggy bank!"

"It's more than we *all* have in our piggy banks," Jessie said.

"I'll call Mrs. McGregor," Benny said, putting the jelly up on the cupboard. "She'll send me my bank and I'll give it to Althea."

Henry stacked plates to rinse before washing. "That's nice of you, Benny, but Althea probably wouldn't take your pennies and nickels."

"How will Grandfather help her raise that much money by Friday?" Violet wanted to know. "It seems impossible."

Henry filled the sink with hot, soapy water. "There's only one way: We have to find the treasure."

"But we don't even know what it is!" Jessie said, shaking the tablecloth out the back door.

"Then we'll just have to look harder," said Benny.

"We'll find it," Violet said confidently. "We can't let Cousin Althea down."

As soon as the dishes were done, the kids dashed upstairs. Yesterday they'd cleaned the small rooms on the third floor. Today they'd work on the second floor.

Jessie yanked back the dusty curtains in the first room. She looked out the window and into the yard below. Althea was talking to Tate. Both had slumped shoulders.

She wondered if Cousin Althea and the gardener were afraid. If Peacock Hall was sold, where would they go? Grandfather was in town again, looking for a way to save Peacock Hall.

The children worked hard for two hours. They also peered behind paintings for hidden wall safes, searched dressers and desks for secret compartments, and tapped inside closets for false backs.

But their hunt turned up only dust bunnies. No treasure.

They were all grimy and tired. They needed a break.

"Let's walk to Heather and David's roadside stand," Jessie suggested. "I'd like parsley for tonight's dinner to go with those new potatoes Grandfather bought."

"Yeah!" Benny agreed. As much as he

liked the big old house, he was glad to go outside.

After washing up, the children set off across the dandelion-spotted field that was a shortcut to the highway.

Benny skipped in the bright green grass. The warm sunshine made him giddy. He plucked a handful of dandelions and tossed them in the air.

Henry smiled at his brother. The soft spring air made him feel like running, too.

"Race you!" he challenged, and the kids were off.

By the time they reached the wooden stand at the side of the highway, they were out of breath and giggling.

Heather Olsen was arranging ivy in a basket. She smiled when she heard the Aldens.

"Looks like you guys have spring fever!" she said.

Benny felt his forehead. "Not me. I'm not sick."

"It's an expression," Henry told him. "It means that people feel good in the springtime."

"What can I do for you today?" Heather asked them.

"I'd like some parsley," said Jessie. "Grandfather bought some new potatoes. I'm going to make parsley potatoes for dinner tonight."

Heather slipped the leafy plant into a plastic bag. "That sounds delicious. I bet you're a good cook."

"We all like to cook," Jessie said.

"But I'd rather eat!" Benny put in.

Violet sniffed. Something fragrant sweetened the air around the stand.

"What is that nice smell?" she asked Heather.

"Lavender. It's often made into sachets, perfumes, and lotions." Heather pointed to a bouquet of dried purple flowers pinned to her sweater. "I wear it all the time."

Violet wondered where David was today. Before she could ask, a shiny black car pulled off the highway.

A woman with stiff blond hair and pink lipstick stepped out of the car.

"Hello," the woman said, stalking across

the gravel in spiky high heels. "I'm Marlene Sanders."

Jessie perked up. The name sounded familiar. Where had she heard it before?

"Hello," Heather greeted. "Welcome to my stand."

"And you are?" Marlene demanded.

"I'm Heather Olsen." The younger woman suddenly seemed very uncomfortable.

Marlene gave a fake smile. "Heather, who sells herbs. How cute. I'll take some basil and thyme."

Heather began measuring snipped leafy herbs into a small silver scale. "Is this enough?"

The woman pinched green stems between fingers tipped with long pink fingernails. "Your herbs *are* fresh?" she asked archly.

"Of course," Heather replied. Nervously, she tied the plastic bag with a strand of brown twine.

Benny also realized Heather's son wasn't around. "Where's David?" he asked.

"He's . . . off on an errand," Heather said, tying the twine into a tight knot.

BASILS

Marlene peeled dollar bills from an expensive leather wallet. "I don't see a business license anywhere." Her tone was disapproving.

"It's at home," Heather said quickly, her face pale. "If you're finished, I have plants to water."

"Of course. But you *do* know licenses must be displayed. It's the law." Marlene Sanders got back into her shiny car and drove off.

Jessie was concerned about Heather. The young woman seemed frightened.

"Are you all right?" she asked.

"I'm fine," Heather said shortly. "I just have a lot of work to do."

Jessie glanced at Henry, who nodded back. It was obvious Heather wanted them to leave.

"We should be going," Jessie said. "Cousin Althea is taking us to Monticello this afternoon."

"Tell David we said hi," Benny said. Then he spotted a boy in a red-striped shirt coming across the field. "There he is! Hey, David!"

As soon as David saw the Aldens, he quickly turned and ran in the opposite direction into the woods.

"What's wrong with *him*?" Benny said.

"He's just shy," Heather told him. "If you're going to Monticello, you'd better hurry back to Peacock Hall."

The children didn't need another hint. When they were well away from Heather's herb stand, they discussed the strange incident.

"David is not shy," Violet stated. "He's avoiding us."

"But why?" Jessie wondered. "We've never done or said anything to upset him."

"Maybe not, but his mother was plenty upset," Henry put in. "Did you see how nervous she was when Marlene Sanders was asking a bunch of nosy questions?"

Jessie scratched her head. "I've heard that woman's name before, but I can't think where. You're right, Henry. Heather definitely acted like she had something to hide."

"*Another* mystery!" Benny crowed. "So

far we have to find the hidden treasure and find out who climbed up to the girls' window —"

"And figure out what's the matter with Heather and David," Violet finished for him. "That's three mysteries and we only have three days."

"One mystery a day," Benny said, counting on his fingers.

Henry ruffled Benny's hair. "You're getting too smart! Pretty soon you'll be solving mysteries all by yourself."

Benny grinned, pleased with his big brother's praise. He would start solving those mysteries right away, just as soon as he had lunch.

For her job at the Jefferson Center for Historic Plants, Cousin Althea wore a long, rosebud-sprigged cotton dress topped with a white apron. A white ruffled cap sat on her curls.

"I love your dress," Violet said as they were driving to Monticello.

"We all wear eighteenth-century costumes," Althea said. "This outfit is fun to wear this time of year, but it's chilly in the fall. Then I put on a shawl."

She pulled into the employee parking lot. "I'll be in there," she said, pointing to a large building. "Roam around all you want. Meet me in the plant center at three-thirty."

Instead of touring the house, the children wandered around the spacious grounds. They took the roundabout walk, bordered with beautiful spring flowers, on the west side of the mansion.

Catching up with a tour group, the Aldens learned that Mr. Jefferson liked to experiment with different kinds of plants.

"He tested over two hundred and fifty varieties of vegetables," the guide stated. "His favorite vegetable was the pea, and he grew twenty kinds of peas in his thousand-foot garden."

Benny wrinkled his nose. He loved to eat, but green peas were not his favorite food. "Twenty kinds of peas! Yuck!"

Teasing him, Jessie said, "We're having peas tonight for dinner!"

"It's almost three-thirty," Henry told them. "We'd better head back to the plant center."

The Center for Historic Plants was enormous, with exhibits, more gardens, and a gift shop where people could buy plants and seeds grown on the estate.

Althea was working behind a cash register. She held up five fingers, meaning she would be ready in five minutes.

Violet wandered around the busy shop. She was browsing through a book on wildflowers when someone bumped into her.

Knocked off balance, Violet stumbled into a rack of seed packets. She caught the stand before it toppled with a crash.

"*Mind your own business,*" a voice whispered hoarsely.

Still grappling with the rack, Violet couldn't turn around to see who had spoken.

But she smelled a familiar scent.

Lavender.

CHAPTER 5

Inside the Old Desk

Henry rushed over when he saw Violet having trouble.

"What happened?" he asked, pushing the stand upright.

"Somebody knocked into me," Violet explained. "And I fell into this."

"Did you see who ran into you?" Henry asked.

She shook her head. "No, but whoever it was whispered, 'Mind your own business.' And I smelled lavender. Like Heather wears."

Henry scanned the room. Since he was taller, he could see over racks and dividers. But the gift shop was packed with customers.

"I don't see Heather. Are you sure it was her?"

"No, I'm not. The voice could have been anybody," Violet said. "But Heather is the only person I know who wears lavender. She told us this morning she wears it all the time."

Jessie and Benny made their way across the crowded room. Henry quickly told them what was going on.

"Would Heather follow us to Monticello?" Jessie wondered.

"You told her we were coming here," Benny reminded her.

"That's right, I did." Jessie frowned. "Even if Heather did bump into Violet, why would she tell Violet to mind her own business? She doesn't even know us."

"Maybe she knows Cousin Althea," Violet said. "Her stand is just across the field."

"Heather *did* give us directions to Peacock Hall," Henry added. "She must know the way to Althea's house very well."

Jessie gave him a nudge. "Here comes Althea now. Let's not tell her about this. She's worried enough about paying her taxes."

They drove back to Peacock Hall. Grandfather's station wagon was parked in the driveway.

"Grandfather is back already," Henry remarked. "I thought he'd be gone all day."

"Maybe he has good news!" Benny said, leaping out of Althea's old car.

But he didn't.

"I'm sorry," James Alden reported to Althea. "I wasn't able to get you an extension. You must pay your back taxes by Friday no later than five o'clock."

Althea raked her fingers through her white curls. She looked so pale, Jessie fetched her a glass of water.

"Thank you, dear." Althea gratefully sipped the cool drink. "And thank you, James. I know you've done all you can. I guess I was hoping for a miracle."

"I'm not finished yet," Grandfather assured her. "I still have a few more people to see."

Althea gave a weak smile. "Don't worry. They'll have to carry me out. That's the only way I'm leaving!"

"Is anybody hungry?" Benny said suddenly.

Violet laughed. "Hint, hint!"

Grandfather laughed, too. "As a matter of fact, I'm starving. Let's all go into town and have supper."

They piled into Grandfather's rental car and drove into Charlottesville. Althea pointed out sights along the way.

"That's the University of Virginia," she said. "Mr. Jefferson founded the University and designed the buildings."

Grandfather pulled the car into the parking lot of a restaurant. "Is this where we're eating?" Jessie asked. "The College Inn?"

"I've had lunch here," Grandfather said. "The food is very good."

"It *is* good," Althea agreed, smiling her thanks as Henry opened the door for her.

"They have terrific ice cream. Did you know Mr. Jefferson served ice cream at Monticello? In those days, ice cream was a real treat."

Inside, Benny sat down and asked the waitress, "You don't have peas here, do you?"

"Only if you want them," the waitress replied, grinning.

"Not really," Benny said. "Did Thomas Jefferson build this building, too?" He was afraid he'd have to eat peas if Mr. Jefferson had founded the College Inn restaurant.

"Not to my knowledge, honey," the waitress said in her soft drawl. "What'll you folks have this evening?"

The children ordered hamburgers, french fries, and milk. Grandfather and Althea decided on large Greek salads and iced tea.

"We'll have some of Mr. Jefferson's famous ice cream for dessert," Althea said, teasing Benny.

"Good idea," Benny said. Ice cream tasted better than peas any day.

Jessie glanced around the room. College students drew up extra chairs to the small tables. She wondered what interesting subjects they were talking about.

Then her gaze fell on a familiar pair. Jessie stiffened when she recognized Marlene Sanders with Roscoe Janney.

Althea saw them, too. "What is my great-nephew doing with that real estate woman?"

"Real estate woman?" Jessie asked. "Do you know her?"

At that moment, Roscoe spotted the Aldens and his great-aunt. He stood up, tossed a few bills on the table, and left the restaurant.

"What's with him?" Henry wanted to know.

"Good question," Althea said. "Roscoe has never been this rude to me before. I wonder —"

If Roscoe Janney was suddenly shy, Marlene Sanders was not. She fixed her lipstick, rubbed some lotion on her hands, then closed her purse. Wearing a phony smile, she came over to their table.

"Mrs. Randolph," she greeted. "Mr. Alden." She didn't look at the Alden children.

"Althea, have you thought over my offer?"

Althea raised her chin. "*Ms.* Sanders, I have no intention of selling Peacock Hall to your firm."

Marlene shook her head. "You're making a big mistake. We've made you a very generous offer. I know for a fact your taxes are due Friday and you don't have the money."

"You don't know everything about my business affairs," Althea stated.

"Well, I do know that on Saturday Peacock Hall will be auctioned and my company will pick it up for a song. And you won't have a dime." With that, Marlene Sanders stalked away.

"That woman almost makes me forget I'm a lady," Althea said.

"She's not very nice," Violet agreed, remembering the way the real estate woman had acted at Heather's stand that morning. She thought she caught a whiff of a sweet fragrance. But the smell of a pizza at the next table was stronger.

Grandfather asked Althea, "Have you considered her offer?"

"As if I'd sell to a company that would turn Peacock Hall into a golf course!" Althea shuddered. "I'd rather be thrown out in the street first."

"But," Grandfather pointed out, "Ms. Sanders's firm will probably buy Peacock Hall anyway."

"Roscoe made an offer, too," Althea said. "But he's not a Randolph. I just hate going against my husband's wishes."

"Maybe you won't have to," said Jessie. "We still have three more days."

The Aldens had solved many mysteries. Jessie knew a lot could happen in three days. If only they had one clue about the secret of Peacock Hall!

Althea smiled. "I'm so glad you all are here. It means the world to me."

"We're glad to help," said Grandfather.

After dinner, they drove back to Peacock Hall. Since the sun was down, the peacocks were quiet. It was too early to go to bed. Henry called his sisters and brother into an emergency meeting.

"We can't afford to waste a minute," he

said. "Let's hunt for the treasure now."

"Good idea," Violet agreed. "Grandfather and Cousin Althea are playing checkers."

"Let's finish the second floor," Jessie said, leading the way up the long staircase. "We still have those back rooms to search."

The back rooms were down the hall from the bedrooms the Aldens were using. The windows were smaller and the furniture was older. One room seemed to be used for storage. It contained several trunks, dressers, and desks.

The children decided to search that room first. They each chose a piece of furniture and began pulling out drawers and checking for secret panels.

Benny sneezed as he opened a trunk.

"We should have cleaned in here first," Jessie murmured. "Benny, be careful with those old clothes. They could be valuable."

Benny held up a long blue satin gown. "Is this the treasure?" He wrinkled his nose at the funny smell. "It stinks, if it is."

Jessie giggled. "Those are mothballs. The

smell is supposed to keep moths from eating holes in stored clothes."

"That *is* a pretty dress," Violet remarked. "Do you think it's worth a lot of money?"

Henry glanced over at the pile of clothing around Benny's ankles. "I doubt the whole trunkful is worth nine thousand dollars. Though a drama company might like to buy those outfits for costumes."

Jessie jiggled at a stubborn catch on the desk by the window. The drawer wouldn't pull free. She tugged harder. It wasn't locked, just rusted shut with time.

Suddenly the drawer yanked loose, sending Jessie backward. She landed on the floor with a thump.

"Are you okay?" asked Henry.

"I'm fine." She glanced at the empty drawer and sighed. "All that for nothing!"

"Maybe not." Benny was staring at a square of yellow paper fluttering to the floor.

CHAPTER 6

Gone!

Jessie scooped up the fragile scrap. "What's this?"

"It fell out of the desk when you pulled the drawer," Benny said.

The others gathered around to examine the paper.

"It looks really old," Henry said, handling the paper carefully. "The writing is faded in some places."

Benny turned his head sideways. "I can't read that funny printing."

"It's not printing," Jessie told him. "In

the old days, people wrote in a fancy way."

The children studied the paper in the lamplight, but no one could make out the wavery writing.

"Let's take it downstairs and show Grandfather," said Jessie. "I bet he can read it."

They ran down the stairs to the living room.

Grandfather was just jumping one of Althea's pieces. "King me," he said. "What have you children got there?"

Jessie handed the yellowed paper to him. "We found this in an old desk. Can you read it?"

Grandfather pushed his glasses up on his nose. "This is very old, judging from the paper and ink. 'Receipt for' . . . something, something . . . 'England.' That's all I can read."

"Let me try," Althea said, adjusting her own glasses. "Is that a date at the bottom? I can't read it any better than you, James."

"It's obviously a receipt for an item. Possibly something bought in England," Grand-

father said. "Do you want to put this away, Althea?"

"Oh, heavens, let the children have it. They found it." Althea rummaged in a drawer and gave Jessie an envelope. "Keep it in this, dear."

Benny jumped up and down. "Is this the treasure?"

"I'm afraid not," Henry said.

Violet felt her little brother's disappointment. "We'll find the treasure, Benny. We'll just keep looking."

"You children are exactly right!" Althea told them. "Tomorrow I'll help you search for that old Randolph treasure. Now you've got me excited about it!"

Grandfather glanced at the mantel clock. "Tomorrow will be here sooner than you think. Run on up to bed and you'll be fresh for the search in the morning."

The children kissed their grandfather and Cousin Althea good night, then went upstairs.

As the clock struck nine, Jessie leaned over the banister to watch the little wooden figures in the clock. There were so many neat things in Peacock Hall.

"We have to save this house," she said solemnly. "We just have to."

The next morning, Grandfather left early for town. Althea cooked breakfast, then insisted on cleaning up.

"You children take a walk before you start poking around this dusty old place. Enjoy the sunshine!"

Henry had an idea. "We'll show Tate the old paper from the desk. Maybe he knows what it is. He's worked here a long time."

Outside they found Tate pulling weeds from the tulip border. Violet admired the colors of the tulips — yellow and bright red. Her fingers itched to paint the scene.

"Hi," Henry said to the old man.

"Oh." The gardener didn't even look up from his task. "It's you kids."

"We want to show you something we found." Jessie pulled the yellowed paper from the envelope she stored it in. "It was in a desk on the second floor. Do you know what it is?"

Tate squinted at the faded paper. "Looks like Latin," he said after a moment. "Never studied Latin. Can't read a word of it."

"It's not Latin," Henry told him. "Grandfather read a few words and they're in English."

Tate handed the paper back to Jessie. "I don't have time for riddles, miss. I've got to get these weeds out before they choke the tulips."

Kneeling, Benny stroked the velvety petal of a yellow tulip. "How come nobody picks these?"

Tate rocked back on his heels. "Good question, young man. In the old days, my flowers would be in vases all over the house. But now it's just Mrs. Randolph and me. And we don't bother cutting flowers. It's all we can do to keep the roof from falling in!"

"Tell us about the old days," Jessie said. "What was it like? Was the yard pretty?"

"Oh, it was grand!" Tate answered, warming to the subject. "And the Randolphs gave fancy parties. At night, the driveway was lined with Japanese lanterns. They sparkled like fireflies!"

"Did a lot of people come?" Violet asked.

"You bet! Roscoe Janney loved to visit. When he was about your age, Benny, he'd follow me around like a puppy dog. He always wanted to live in Peacock Hall."

Benny couldn't believe Roscoe Janney was ever *his* age! Cousin Althea's great-nephew was no fun at all!

"Do you know anything about the treasure?" Henry asked.

Tate bent to his chore again. "I don't have time for foolishness."

Henry wondered why the old man was friendly one minute and unfriendly the next.

Benny wandered over to the empty fish pond. Climbing over the crumbling ledge, he stood next to the goldfish fountain. The statue stood on its tail. Water was supposed to spout from the open mouth.

Rubbing his fingers over the carved scales, Benny felt something. He looked closer.

Two letters had been scratched in the granite — *R.J.*

Roscoe Janney.

"Look what I found!" he cried, waving the others over.

"I bet those are Roscoe Janney's initials," Henry said.

"Good work, Benny," Violet said. "That proves what Tate was saying — that Roscoe came here a lot when he was a kid."

"But why would he carve his initials on the fish statue?" Benny wondered.

Henry replied, "It's a way of saying, 'I was here.' "

Violet touched the marks on the statue. "I wonder if this was Roscoe's way of saying, 'This is mine.' "

Jessie remembered the way Roscoe had guiltily left the restaurant last night. "You may have a point, Violet. I bet Roscoe is up to something. He seems to want to buy Peacock Hall pretty badly. Tate said Roscoe loved the house."

"Do you think Tate was our prowler?" Violet asked. "He has ladders and things in his garden shed."

Jessie pulled the scrap of denim from her pocket. "We still don't know about those jeans on the clothesline. They might be hanging up now. I'd like to compare this piece of material to the hole."

Henry nodded.

The children hurried across the lawn to the smokehouse. The peacock was scratching around the pen, but paid no attention to the Aldens.

"Why won't the big one put his tail up?" Benny asked. He still longed to have a peacock feather.

"He only does it to show off in front of the peahen," Jessie replied. "And she's not around."

"Well, he could show off in front of *us*," Benny said.

Henry laughed. "I think he does, sometimes. Peacocks are vain birds. They like to be admired."

Benny wondered if the peacock knew the secret of the house. After all, the place was named after the bird.

By now they had rounded the corner of the smokehouse. Sure enough, clean laundry flapped in the spring breeze.

Violet stared at the clothes pegged to the line. Shirts, jeans, socks — all for someone about her size.

"That shirt," she said suddenly. "The red-striped one near the end — David was wearing it when he ran from us."

"You're right!" Jessie exclaimed. "These are David's clothes! I wonder why David's laundry is hanging on a line at Tate's house."

Just then Tate himself hustled around the corner.

"What are you kids doing around this place? Didn't I tell you to stay away?"

"We just —" Benny began.

But Tate wouldn't let him finish. "Go on!" he yelled. "You don't have any business around here!"

"Let's go," Henry said to the others. There was no point in arguing. Tate would only get angrier, he figured. "There's only one way to clear up this mystery."

Violet caught on instantly. "Go back to Heather's stand! She can tell us why David's clothes are here."

It didn't take them long to hike across the dandelion-dotted field.

But the stand was deserted.

No wreaths decorated the front, no bunches of fragrant herbs hung invitingly from the rafters. Heather and David were nowhere in sight.

"They're gone!" Violet cried.

Jessie ran her hand over the board counter. "It's as if they were never here. What happened to them?"

"They must be in Tate's smokehouse," Henry concluded.

"David's *clothes* are at the smokehouse," Jessie corrected. "We don't know where Heather and David are."

Henry turned toward the path across the field. "We don't have time to solve this mystery. Not if we want to help Cousin Althea keep Peacock Hall."

Grandfather was pulling into the driveway as the children crossed the lawn.

"You look like you have news," he said to them.

"We do," said Henry. "We went to Heather's stand, but it's empty. And Heather and David are gone."

Grandfather sighed. "I saw Heather Olsen at the courthouse earlier today. She was arguing with someone in the license bureau. Apparently she doesn't have a business license and someone reported her to the county. County officials shut down her stand."

Jessie glanced at Violet. They knew who reported Heather — nosy Marlene Sanders.

"So she's out of business?" Henry asked.

"Until she obtains a proper license, I'm afraid so," Grandfather said.

Benny frowned. "But that's not fair. I like Heather."

"I like her, too," Grandfather said. "But some things in life aren't fair."

Jessie glanced up at Peacock Hall. Cousin Althea was on the verge of losing her home. And they were running out of time. Some things were definitely *not* fair.

As if reading his sister's mind, Benny said, "Let's get back to looking for the treasure. Today we'll find it!"

As they went into the house, Violet said, "We have so many things to look for — Heather and David, the treasure. And all we've found is an old piece of paper nobody can read!"

"Let's see the paper again, Jessie," Henry said.

Jessie pulled out the envelope. "I still can't make heads or tails out of it."

"Heads or tails?" Benny echoed.

"It's an expression," Jessie explained. "It means it's a mystery to me!"

"What's a mystery?" boomed a voice from the doorway.

The Aldens looked up to see Roscoe Janney striding into the room.

"What's a mystery?" the young man repeated, smiling.

Jessie didn't trust that smile. "Uh — nothing," she said, slipping the old receipt into a drawer behind her.

Henry knew what she was doing. "We

were just wondering why the sun comes up in the east," he said as a distraction. "It's a mystery to us!"

"Not really. You see, the earth rotates around the sun —" Then Roscoe laughed. "It's too nice a day to think about science. That's why I came by."

"Why *did* you come by?" Althea asked, entering the room with Grandfather.

"To take you and your guests on an outing," Roscoe said. "To Natural Bridge! It'll be fun!"

"I guess that'll be all right," Grandfather said.

Henry was suspicious of Roscoe Janney. He was too nice, all of a sudden. Did Roscoe see Jessie hide the receipt?

If Roscoe was with them on a trip, he couldn't do any harm, Henry decided.

But the Aldens would keep an eye on Althea's great-nephew.

CHAPTER 7

Who Robbed Peacock Hall?

The sight of Roscoe Janney's car made Henry's pulse beat faster. Roscoe owned a big old Jeep.

"Do you go camping?" he asked Roscoe. He still didn't trust the guy, but he admired that cool car.

"I used to," Roscoe replied. "The Jeep is great over these mountains in the winter."

Grandfather climbed into the bucket seat next to the driver. Althea and the girls sat in the backseat. Benny and Henry got into the rear compartment, where jump seats had been installed.

Roscoe proved to be the perfect travel guide. He told funny stories about the region. He pointed out deer poised by the roadside and red-tailed hawks perched on phone wires.

Althea was quiet on the drive. Jessie wondered why she came on this trip, since she and Roscoe didn't get along.

Benny wondered why they were taking the trip at all. What was so special about a bridge? When they finally arrived, he was surprised.

Benny expected to see a metal bridge. Instead, he saw a huge stone rock with a hole in it.

"That's the bridge?" he asked.

"That's it," replied Roscoe. He drove over the rock formation, which spanned Cedar Creek. Then he parked the Jeep and they all got out.

"I wish I had brought my camera," Violet said. "But at least I have the drawing tablet Cousin Althea gave me."

"A sketch would be nice," Grandfather told her. "I was here once before, but it was a long time ago."

Roscoe told the Aldens about the limestone formation.

"The bridge is one of the seven natural wonders of the world," he recited.

Althea took over. "Thomas Jefferson was so awed by it, he bought it from King George the Third for twenty shillings."

"How much?" asked Benny.

"Not very much money," Roscoe put in. "Considering property prices these days." He gave his aunt a meaningful glance. Althea frowned.

"Can we explore?" Henry asked Grandfather.

"Go ahead. It's perfectly safe," Grandfather said. "We'll go into the café."

The children ran to the overlook and gazed down.

Violet propped her drawing pad on the rock ledge and began sketching the ancient arch.

Behind them, a tour guide with his group was saying, "In 1750, a young man named

George Washington surveyed the bridge. If you look on the southwest wall, you'll find his initials."

Benny became excited. More initials! "Can we go see George Washington's initials?" he asked.

"Sure," said Jessie. "Let's follow the group."

They hiked down the path to the inside of the arch.

"There it is!" Benny cried, pointing up high to a box carved into the limestone. With his keen eyes, he could see the letters *G.W.*

Then the children joined the grown-ups in the café. Roscoe treated them to ice-cream cones. He kept looking at his watch, Henry noticed. Why was Roscoe so concerned about the time? He didn't seem to be in a rush.

On their way back to Peacock Hall, Benny borrowed a sheet of Violet's drawing paper. He wrote *B.A.* over and over. Writing the letters reminded him of something, but he couldn't figure out what.

Roscoe pulled the Jeep behind Grandfather's station wagon. "Here we are," he said cheerfully. "I hope you all had a nice time."

"Yes, we did," said Jessie. "Thank you for taking us." As she climbed out, she saw Roscoe's hands shaking on the steering wheel.

"I won't come in this time," he said to Althea.

"I wasn't going to invite you," she said tartly. "It's late and the children need their supper."

Before the Aldens and Althea reached the porch, Roscoe backed the Jeep around and roared down the driveway.

"Boy, he's sure in a hurry," Benny commented.

"I'm glad he didn't stay." Althea fumbled with her keys, but the door was open slightly. "That's odd. I'm sure I locked the door behind me."

They all walked down the hall and into the living room. Althea gave a little scream.

Every piece of furniture had been overturned. Cushions lay scattered on the floor. The stern-faced portraits hung crookedly on the walls.

"I've been robbed!" Althea moaned. "James, call the police at once!"

"Let's make sure no one is still in the house," said Grandfather. He and Henry checked the big place.

When they returned, Henry reported, "Nothing was messed up in any of the other rooms. Only this room."

"Maybe we surprised the burglar," Althea said. "He tried to get in the night you all arrived, remember."

"But we didn't see anybody run out," Violet pointed out. "And no one's hiding in the house or Grandfather would have found him. Or her."

Henry had a theory. "I think whoever broke in was after one particular thing. And that person knew exactly which room to look in. This one."

"There's nothing of value in here," Althea said. "What could anybody possibly want that was in my living room?"

Jessie felt a chill down her spine. The receipt! They'd been studying it when Roscoe Janney came in earlier. She'd slipped it into a drawer behind her. Was it there now?

Jessie walked over to the small table. The contents of the drawer — postcards and letters — were strewn on the floor. She pawed through the papers.

"It's not here!" she cried.

"What's not here?" asked Grandfather.

Henry knew at once. "The old receipt we found. We were looking at it when Roscoe came in today. Jessie hid it in the drawer so he wouldn't see it. But he did see!"

"But how could Roscoe steal the receipt?" Benny asked. "He was with us on the trip!"

"I didn't think that old piece of paper was important," said Althea.

"Apparently it is," Grandfather said. "Or else someone wouldn't have gone to the trouble to steal it. Do you still want to call the police?"

Althea shook her head. "As long as nothing else is missing . . ." She sighed. "Anyway, the sheriff will be out here soon enough. To throw me out."

When the adults left the room, the children huddled together.

"Who could have broken in?" Jessie asked.

"It couldn't have been Roscoe," Henry said. "Unless he had a friend break in."

"What about Tate?" Benny brought up. "Roscoe and Tate are friends."

Jessie bit her lip. "Tate's kind of weird, but I think he's loyal to Althea. I don't think he'd rob her."

Henry agreed with Benny. "We can't rule him out as a suspect."

"Is the old paper a clue to the treasure?" Violet asked what they all were thinking.

Now they'd never know.

The next morning, Grandfather left for town, again hoping to turn up some legal information that would help Althea.

"Tomorrow is the last day," he said.

Althea had to go to Monticello. "I have the early shift," she told the children.

"We'll stay here and look for the treasure," Benny said.

Althea shook her head. "I'm sorry, Benny, but I can't allow you children to stay here alone. Not after what happened last night."

"But Tate is around," Violet reminded her.

Althea shook her head. "I know, but I'd feel better if you were with me. You can search the house this afternoon."

Was she suspicious of the gardener, too? Jessie wondered.

This time the children toured Jefferson's home again. They located their favorite inventions, one by one.

"Now for mine," said Benny, heading for the dining room.

A guide was just demonstrating the dumbwaiters built into the fireplace that Jefferson used for meals.

"I still wish I had a little elevator in my room," said Benny.

Henry laughed. "Just what you need, Benny Alden. Twenty-four-hour room service!"

At last Cousin Althea's shift was over. They all drove back to Peacock Hall.

"Let's start searching," Benny said, rushing upstairs.

"But you haven't had lunch yet!" Jessie called.

Benny hurried back down the stairs. "Okay, but let's make it quick."

"Boy, you *must* be anxious to find the treasure," Violet teased.

Althea understood the children's eagerness. "Go ahead," she urged. "I'll bring lunch up on a tray."

"Too bad you don't have one of those waiter elevators," Benny remarked. "Then you wouldn't have to walk upstairs."

"It's very unusual for houses to have dumbwaiters," Althea said, chuckling.

Lunch was a tasty combination of cold chicken sandwiches and potato salad. Cold lemonade quenched their thirst after working in dusty rooms.

But after searching for several hours, the children didn't find the secret of Peacock Hall. They trudged downstairs to help Althea with dinner. Grandfather called and said he would be late. He was meeting with an old lawyer friend.

While they were washing dishes, a familiar voice called.

"Anybody home?" Roscoe Janney walked

confidently into the kitchen. "Hello, Auntie."

"Hello, Roscoe." Althea didn't seem pleased to see her great-nephew.

"I came by to make you my final offer," Roscoe said, getting straight to business. He pulled out a typewritten sheet. "Here it is. Take it or leave it."

Althea barely glanced at the sheet. "I'm not that desperate."

"Yes, you are. Tomorrow is your last day. If you don't pay your taxes, you'll lose Peacock Hall," Roscoe said.

"I still have one more day," Althea said firmly.

Roscoe laughed, stuffing the paper back in his pocket. "You'll be sorry you didn't take me up on my offer!"

"This is still my house, Roscoe Janney," Althea said, trying to control her anger. "Please leave at once."

Whistling, Roscoe left.

"I don't trust that guy," Henry said to the other children. "Let's make sure he really leaves."

CHAPTER 8

The Figure at the Window

The Aldens ran upstairs to a room with windows that overlooked the front lawn.

"This is where we found the old paper," Benny said.

"And now it's gone," Violet added.

Henry went over to the windows. Roscoe was standing by the empty goldfish pond. He glanced around, as if waiting for someone.

"I wonder who he's waiting for," Henry said.

Jessie and the others joined Henry,

pulling the dusty draperies back so they could see.

Then an older man joined Roscoe. It was Tate.

Violet watched the two men. "They seem awfully happy."

"Tate did say Roscoe came here a lot when he was a kid," Henry said. "I guess they're still good friends. But how can Tate be laughing when he's about to lose his home? Where will he go?"

Jessie wasn't listening. From here, she had a good view of the smokehouse. A light shone in the single window.

"Look!" she cried.

A small figure passed in front of the window. Who was it?

"Somebody's in the smokehouse," Violet said.

"Whoever it is, Tate doesn't want anyone to know," Jessie said, remembering the times Tate had scolded them.

"But he's busy with Roscoe," Henry pointed out. "We could go out the back way and he'd never see us. We could find out who Tate's mysterious guest is."

Benny was already heading for the door. "Let's go!"

The back staircase came out by the kitchen. As the children tiptoed past the hallway, they glimpsed Cousin Althea sitting alone in the living room.

Violet felt sorry for her. If only Grandfather would come back with good news!

The lawn was damp with dew. Violet's sneakers were soaked by the time they reached the smokehouse. Above the piney woods a round moon was rising. It was an evening for surprises, she thought.

Benny peered into the peacock pen. Both birds were roosting on the roof of the little house. At least the peacock's cry wouldn't give them away.

He took the lead as they crept single file around the corner of the smokehouse.

The front door was open!

Benny was ready to charge in when Henry pulled him back.

"Let me go first," Henry whispered. "I'll make sure it's safe."

Cautiously he stuck his head inside the door.

"Might as well come in," called a young voice.

Violet knew that voice. "David!" she exclaimed, rushing past Henry and inside the little building.

David sat on an old chair at a table. He'd been reading a book. He wore a pair of jeans with a hole in one knee.

"Mom's out," he said quietly. "She's picking flowers to finish an order."

Violet gazed around the small room. Bunches of dried herbs and flowers hung from the wooden ceiling beams. Fresh flowers stood in buckets and canning jars of water. An herb wreath lay on a larger table. Dishes stacked in the tiny sink and a basket of folded laundry were the final clues.

"You and your mother live here!" she declared. "You're the secret Tate's been keeping from us!"

David sighed. "That's right." He indicated a worn-out sofa and another old chair. "I knew you four wouldn't give up till you found out the truth. Sit down, everyone."

When the Aldens made themselves comfortable, David began his story.

"Mom and I lost our lease back last fall. The lease on our apartment," he explained. "Our landlord raised the rent. Mom couldn't pay it, so we had to leave. But we didn't have anyplace to go."

Jessie felt a pang of sympathy. "We know what you mean. When our parents died, we didn't have a home, either."

"So we moved into an old boxcar," Henry said. "And that's where we lived till Grandfather found us and took us to live with him."

"I wish I had a grandfather like yours," David said wistfully. "But it's just Mom and me. Most of the time we get along pretty good. But this past winter . . ." He stopped.

Violet thought David looked as if he was going to cry. "How did you meet Tate?" she asked gently.

"He was driving along the highway and he saw us walking. He stopped to give us a ride. When he found out we didn't have anyplace to live, he said we were coming home with him and he wouldn't take no for an answer." David smiled at the memory. "Tate can be pretty bossy sometimes."

"Why didn't he tell Cousin Althea?" Henry wanted to know. "Why is he keeping you and your mother a secret?"

"Tate was going to tell Mrs. Randolph. But then Mrs. Randolph got that tax letter, and Tate thought she had enough to worry about. So he never told her about us."

"Were you going to live here forever?" Benny asked. He liked the smokehouse. It was small and neat, like their boxcar.

David shook his head. "Mom opened the herb stand on the highway. She was saving money to get us an apartment in town. But then the county made her shut down her stand. I don't know what's going to happen now."

The children were silent a moment.

Jessie absently pulled the scrap of denim from the pocket of her skirt.

"What's that?" David asked.

Jessie flushed. "It's a piece of material. We saw your pants hanging on the clothesline and wondered if the material came from your jeans."

As if to answer her question, David got up and opened a bureau drawer. He pulled out two pairs of denim pants, both with holes in the knees. "These belong to my mom. She can't afford to buy us new clothes."

Jessie felt worse than ever. "I'm sorry. I didn't mean —"

"We aren't being nosy," Henry put in. "We found the material on the ledge beneath the girls' bedroom window. Somebody tried to break in the first night we got here. He — or she — tore their pants getting away."

David's eyes widened. "You don't think I did it? Or my mother?"

"No, of course not!" Violet said quickly. "But that was before we knew you and Heather lived here in the smokehouse."

Jessie stuffed the scrap back in her pocket. "We keep finding clues, but they lead nowhere."

"I might be able to help," David told her. "You all came here Sunday evening?"

"That's right." Henry leaned forward with interest. "What do you know about that night, David?"

"It was warm and I was out taking a walk," David replied. "Tate told Mom and me that Mrs. Randolph's relatives were coming, so we'd have to stay out of sight."

"Did you see something?" Violet asked anxiously. This was one mystery she definitely wanted solved.

David shook his head. "I didn't see anything, but I heard something. A car with a loud engine."

"Whose car was it?" asked Jessie.

But Henry already knew. A certain Jeep had a powerful engine. "It was Roscoe Janney, wasn't it?"

"Only one car around here that sounds like his Jeep," David said. "He must have parked it along the road instead of in the driveway, so nobody would see him. He probably walked up the driveway."

Henry nodded. This made sense. "Roscoe is friends with Tate, so he could have easily borrowed a ladder from the gardener. But why would he break into his aunt's house?"

Jessie spoke up. "Roscoe knew we were here. Maybe he tried to scare us away."

"But we don't scare that easily," Benny said.

Violet explained to David that they had been involved in several mysteries.

"But this mystery is the hardest of all," she concluded. "We need to find the hidden treasure to save Peacock Hall. So far we don't even know what it is, much less *where* it is."

"Soon Cousin Althea will be without a home," Jessie added. "And Tate. Where will they go?"

Then she realized that David and Heather wouldn't have a home, either, if Peacock Hall was auctioned for taxes.

Now the Aldens had to help *two* families find a home.

In one day.

CHAPTER 9

The Eye of the Peacock

The cry of the peacock awakened Benny early Friday morning.

"It's the last day!" he cried, leaping out of bed.

"I know," Henry said. He threw back his quilt and jumped up. "We have a lot to do."

A knock sounded at their door.

"Come in," Benny called, already dressed.

Violet and Jessie stood in the doorway.

"Ready to search?" Jessie asked, but she knew the answer. If there was anything the Aldens enjoyed, it was a challenge.

"Got to eat first," Benny said sensibly. "We can't hunt for the secret on an empty stomach." He sounded so serious, the others laughed as they went downstairs.

Althea fixed them pancakes with link sausages. "You just missed your grandfather," she said. "He had an early breakfast, then left to go to the bank."

"Is he going to borrow the tax money?" Henry asked.

"He's going to try," Althea said. "My cousin Celia certainly married a nice man. I'm so glad you all are here. No matter what happens."

"You'll have many more days in this house," Jessie said. *If we find the secret of Peacock Hall in time*, she thought.

Althea wouldn't hear of them cleaning up, so the children ran upstairs.

An hour later, they had searched every square inch of the bedrooms they and Grandfather were using.

"I don't suppose this is the treasure," Benny said, producing a bent gold cuff link.

Henry studied the object in better light. "It's not even real gold."

"The only room left up here is Cousin Althea's," Jessie said. "We'd better ask permission first."

She and Violet went downstairs to the kitchen.

Althea listened to their request. "Certainly you may look in my bedroom. But I think I would have found the secret if it were in my own room! I've lived in this house for more than fifty years!"

"She has a point," Violet said to Jessie as they went back upstairs. "Althea must know this place better than anyone. Why hasn't she found the treasure?"

"Maybe because she doesn't know what she's looking for," Jessie brought up. "That's been *our* main problem."

The children felt shy in Althea's bedroom. They looked quickly.

But, as in the other rooms, their search proved fruitless.

Hot, dirty, and tired, they went downstairs.

Althea took one glance at their grimy

faces and poured them glasses of lemonade.

"You are a sight," she pronounced. "Benny even has cobwebs in his hair. Go outside. It's a gorgeous day, but it may not last. Spring can be fickle around here."

"We really can't afford to waste time," Henry said earnestly. "It's lunchtime now. Only five more hours until . . ." He hated to finish the sentence.

Althea waved an unconcerned hand. "You children shouldn't take on my worries. You are guests in my house, even if it is the last day as *my* house."

"Let's all go outside," Jessie suggested, "and eat lunch by the fish pond."

"Wonderful!" Althea agreed.

As they made a lunch of tuna salad sandwiches, bananas, and peanut-butter cookies, everyone's spirits lifted. By the time Henry had spread an old blanket on the grass near the fish pond, they were all laughing at Benny.

"Benny, you know you can't turn a cartwheel!" Violet giggled, watching her little brother tumble in the grass.

"Wait!" he cried. "I'll get it *this* time!"

But he sprawled on the lawn, collapsed in giggles.

As Althea passed the sandwiches around, a shiny blue car pulled into the driveway.

Marlene Sanders got out, carrying a briefcase. She smiled when she saw Althea Randolph sitting on the blanket.

"Lovely day, isn't it?" she said to the older woman. "What glorious weather for your last picnic at Peacock Hall!"

"Can I help you, Ms. Sanders?" Althea inquired formally.

"Yes, you can sign these papers." Marlene Sanders put her briefcase on the edge of the goldfish pond and opened the brass clasp. She took out some long typewritten pages.

"What papers?" Althea asked.

"For the sale of your property." Uncapping a pen, Marlene handed it to Althea.

Althea pushed the papers and pen away. "You don't take no for an answer, do you?"

Marlene sighed. "It would be so much easier this way, Mrs. Randolph. You'd make a lot of money and could find a nice place in Charlottesville."

"I'd rather live in the peacock pen than let your company turn this place into a golf course!" Althea said angrily. "Please go. It *is* still my property!"

"But only till five o'clock!" Marlene said, stuffing the papers back into her leather briefcase. Her high heels clipped smartly along the walk as she marched to her car.

"That woman doesn't give up," Althea murmured, watching the car leave. "I'm sorry she spoiled our picnic."

"It's okay," Jessie told her. "*We* don't give up, either! We still have almost five hours to look for the treasure."

As they ate, dark clouds rolled in. The air turned chilly.

"That awful woman brought bad weather with her," Althea joked.

After helping carry the picnic things back indoors, the children resumed their search on the first floor.

"Let's start in the living room," Henry suggested. "It's the biggest room. It'll take us the longest."

"Can we build a fire?" Violet suggested, shivering. Even though she was wearing a sweater, the room was cold.

Henry nodded. "Benny, let's get some wood."

Tate's woodpile was by the garage, but the boys saw no sign of the gardener. Henry wondered if the old man had gone to town to find a place to live.

"Is this enough?" Benny asked him. He could barely carry the large stack.

"Great. Now let's hurry back inside."

The girls had already pulled back the fireplace grate. Henry knelt and began stacking logs.

Benny, who couldn't see where he was going, tripped over a chair leg. His pile of wood went flying.

"Oh, no!" he cried as a stick hit the right side of the fireplace mantel. "Did it hurt anything?"

Violet peered at the corner of the wood paneling. "There's a scratch in the paint, that's all —" But as she spoke, a piece of carved molding fell to the floor. "Uh-oh!"

Henry picked up the molding with its circular carvings. "I bet we can glue this back —" He stopped, staring in amazement.

The corner of the fireplace slowly creaked open, revealing dark, dusty space inside.

Violet gasped.

"A secret room!" Benny exclaimed, hopping up and down. "We found a secret room! I bet the treasure is in there! Where's my flashlight?"

Jessie had it. She shone the beam inside the space. "It's completely empty!" she cried, disappointed.

"How can it be empty?" Violet demanded. "Did someone find the treasure before us?"

At that moment, the peacock called outside.

"Oh, be quiet," Benny told the bird. If the peacock knew the secret of Peacock Hall, he wasn't much help.

Henry still gazed at the fireplace. What did that panel remind him of? Something he'd seen . . . and then it hit him.

"This is like the fireplace at Monticello!" he declared.

"The little elevators!" Benny said, remembering the dumbwaiters.

Jessie was caught up in the excitement. "Then there's a matching panel on the other side! Let's look!"

"Do we have to hit it with a stick of wood to get it to open?" Benny wondered.

Henry smiled. "I doubt it. That would be a pretty awkward way to get into those secret rooms."

Violet was studying the ovals carved into the molding. "Benny, you were right! The peacock *did* have the answer!"

"What do you mean?" Benny asked.

"This mantel has 'eyes' like the peacock's tail," she replied. "I bet there's a hidden catch in one of these circles." Gently, she pushed the molding.

A door popped open.

Holding her breath, Jessie shone the flashlight inside the cavity. "I'm afraid to look!"

Benny wasn't. He leaned in and pulled out a white china vase with flowers and birds painted all over.

"Ohhh," Violet gasped. "I bet it's worth a lot of money."

Henry saluted his little brother. "Benny Alden, I do believe you've found the Randolph treasure. And with time to spare! It's only two o'clock!"

"The peacock helped, too. We just couldn't figure out what he was saying." Benny frowned at the vase. "Is this really the treasure? It's just an old —"

At that moment, a figure rushed through the doorway.

"I'll take that, thank you!" Roscoe Janney snatched the vase from Benny.

"Hey!" Benny cried. "That belongs to the house!"

"Which will be mine by the end of the day." Roscoe held the vase high out of reach. "And everything in it will be mine, including this vase."

Violet felt a rush of anger. "Cousin Althea doesn't want to sell the house to you!"

"It's either that or be evicted," Roscoe said, shrugging. "I know Aunt Althea. She'll never allow the sheriff to cart her by the road."

"We found that vase," Henry told the young man evenly. "You don't have any claim on it."

"I've been coming to this house ever since I was Benny's age," Roscoe admitted. "I never found the secret of Peacock Hall. But you kids did in less than a week! In fact, you messed up my search the other night."

"That *was* you at the window!" Violet accused.

"I'd been sneaking in here whenever I wanted. I didn't know which bedrooms you were in, and I tried to break into the wrong one." He grinned. "A little mistake."

Suddenly a voice snarled behind him. "Well, don't make any more mistakes, Roscoe Janney!"

Roscoe whirled in surprise.

The priceless vase slipped out of his hands.

CHAPTER 10

Benny Remembers Something

Everyone watched in stunned amazement as the vase hit the floor and smashed into shards.

"Look what you did!" the woman screeched at Roscoe.

"What *I* did!" he yelled back. "You made me drop it!"

Before she turned around, Violet smelled the sweet aroma of lavender. Then she recognized Marlene Sanders's sharp voice.

"You were the one who pushed me in the gift shop," she said to Marlene. "I thought it was Heather Olsen, but you wear lavender, too. It's in your hand lotion."

"So what if I did?" Marlene flared. "You kids are constantly poking into things that aren't any of your business."

Benny stared at the vase, the secret of Peacock Hall, smashed on the floor. All their searching and looking, now in a million pieces.

Althea rushed into the room. "What's all this shouting —" She stopped when she saw her great-nephew and Marlene Sanders. "What's going on here?"

Roscoe jerked his head toward the open panels on either side of the fireplace. "These kids found what I've been looking for since I was their age."

"You still *act* like a kid," Althea said coldly. Then she went over to examine an unlatched door. "Very clever. Like the panels in the dining room at Monticello. Maybe Zachary Randolph had the design copied here at Peacock Hall."

"Benny discovered the secret door," Henry told her. "We were putting wood in the fireplace and he accidently hit the panel."

"We didn't find anything in the first one." Jessie took up the story. "But we figured there must be one on the other side. When we opened it, there was a vase inside."

"Obviously worth a fortune," Marlene snapped, glaring at Roscoe. "And this idiot dropped it!"

Now Roscoe turned on her. "Why did you have to barge in? I took everyone to Natural Bridge so the house would be empty and you could steal that old piece of paper. If you had waited until later like we planned, we'd have the vase *and* the house!"

Marlene dug furiously in her handbag and pulled out the yellowed receipt. "Here! A lot of good this does us now! Without the vase, this is worthless!"

The paper fluttered like a feather to the floor near Benny's feet. He picked it up. He still couldn't read the funny writing. Then he tilted his head and suddenly the two marks at the bottom made sense.

He remembered what had been sticking in his mind the last few days.

The final clue.

Roscoe and Marlene were still arguing.

"You bungler!" she yelled at him. "Who climbed into the wrong window the other night?"

"You thought I should search one last time," Roscoe said. "I practically broke my neck when that kid saw me."

Althea was shocked. "You've been sneaking into my house, Roscoe Janney?"

"So what?" Marlene said. "The plan is ruined."

At that moment Grandfather came in, followed by Tate.

"You're right," Grandfather announced. "Your plan *is* ruined. Althea, I found out from my lawyer friend that your great-nephew and this woman have been plotting together all along."

"To buy my house?" Althea asked. "They've both made me separate offers, but I've always refused."

"Roscoe figured you'd give in before the

deadline," Grandfather explained. "He was counting on your desperation to accept his ridiculously low offer."

"How does this woman fit in?" Althea asked.

"Roscoe was going to turn right around and sell Peacock Hall to my development company at a huge profit," Marlene confessed. "We'd split the profit. Whatever the treasure was, we'd split that, too."

Tate stared at Roscoe, astonished. "I thought you loved this house! When you were little, you talked about living at Peacock Hall. And you were going to sell it?"

"Who wants this old place?" Roscoe said.

Jessie suspected Roscoe was embarrassed at being caught. And he didn't like it that a six-year-old had discovered the secret he had been looking for all these years.

"Now I know why my husband insisted I sell this house to a member of the Randolph family," Althea said to Roscoe. "He must have known you wouldn't love the house."

"Roscoe only loves money," Marlene said.

"You'd better leave," Althea ordered the

real estate woman. "I wouldn't sell to your development firm or my good-for-nothing nephew for the world."

Roscoe stalked into the hall. He made a big show of holding the door open for Marlene Sanders, but she brushed past him angrily.

"I can open my own door!" she said.

After Roscoe had left, Althea glanced at the clock on the mantel. "I'd better pack. It's nearly five. The sheriff will be here soon to escort me off my property."

"That won't be necessary," said Grandfather.

Althea turned, her eyes anxious. "What do you mean? That porcelain vase is in a million pieces. The treasure of Peacock Hall can't help me now."

"Althea, I'm surprised at you! A history expert," Grandfather teased. "The vase was undoubtedly valuable, but you're overlooking the true treasure of Peacock Hall."

Henry understood immediately. "The panels in the fireplace! They're just like the one designed by Thomas Jefferson at Monticello! How many other houses have secret panels hidden in the fireplace? Maybe Thomas Jefferson built these, too!"

"Why, the treasure has been in front of me all these years!" Althea said in awe. "It's very possible Mr. Jefferson designed these fireplace panels. He and Zachary Randolph were friends as well as neighbors."

"Yeah," Benny put in. "He even wrote a note to Zachary."

"What?" Violet asked. "Benny, what are you talking about?"

He held out the paper Marlene had thrown on the floor.

"This," he said. "It's a note from Thomas Jefferson. See? There are his initials in the corner."

Grandfather took the receipt from Benny. "Benny is absolutely right! Talk about not seeing what's right in front of us!"

"I just kept looking at that paper," Benny explained. "And suddenly I could read those two letters at the bottom. *T* and *J*. Like the letters Roscoe wrote on the fish fountain."

"And George Washington carved on the

wall of Natural Bridge!" Jessie added, excited. "Ever since Grandfather got your letter, Althea, Benny has been seeing initials! It all began with your monogrammed letter."

"You children clearly take after your grandmother's side of the family," Althea declared, winking at Grandfather. "Your grandfather is pretty smart, too. I hope he can figure out a way I can keep my house."

"The answer is right here," Grandfather said, waving the receipt. "This little piece of paper is worth a small fortune. It's a receipt for the vase Jefferson brought back from England. Zachary or his wife may have asked Jefferson to buy them some English china. Jefferson wrote this receipt and initialed it."

"That's worth money?" asked Violet.

"People who collect autographs would pay a great deal of money for anything with Jefferson's signature." Grandfather smiled at Althea. "Maybe the foundation that runs Monticello would buy the receipt. It's worth more than enough to pay your taxes."

"It's not too late?" Jessie asked. The clock's hands had nearly crept to five.

"The sheriff is probably on his way," Tate said, mopping his forehead with a handkerchief. "What'll we do when he gets here? He won't care about any old piece of paper."

Grandfather nodded. "I've spent most of this week down at the courthouse. Believe me, the county would much rather have its tax money than go through an eviction procedure. I'm sure you will be granted an extension, Althea, once the news of this discovery is out. And then the autograph buyers will be calling. You'll sell it and have money left over."

Althea sank into a chair. "I can't believe it. I don't know how to thank you, James. And you children!"

"Your problems aren't completely over," Grandfather pointed out gently. "You still need help with this house. And the money left over from the sale of the Jefferson receipt won't last forever."

Tate cleared his throat. "I think I can

help with this problem, Mrs. Randolph." He went to the front door and signaled with his arm.

Heather and David Olsen walked in.

"Who are these people?" Althea asked Tate.

"Heather ran the herb stand on the highway," Benny supplied.

Tate added sheepishly, "I've been letting them stay in the smokehouse. They don't have anyplace to live."

Heather said, "Tate's been wonderful, Mrs. Randolph. We knew it was wrong to stay on your property without your permission, but we just had no place else to go. I had to think about my son."

"How long has this been going on?" asked Althea.

"About two months," Tate answered. "I found them walking along the highway and brought them home. I've been bunking in the dairy house. I hope you're not mad."

"No, Tate, I'm not angry. But I don't like being fooled." Althea's face softened. "Still,

I understand how you must feel, Heather, trying to raise your son."

Heather became excited. "Do you know you have a wonderful herb garden? It's all grown over, but I can bring it back. We could open an herb shop right here at Peacock Hall. Since it's on the way to Monticello, we'd have lots of visitors."

"You could open the house as a public attraction," Grandfather suggested to Althea. "People would love to see that fireplace. Peacock Hall should be registered as an historic property. That way the house will be protected."

"I can help you do that," Heather told Althea. "I know a lot about old houses and gardens."

Althea liked the idea. "You and David could live here, of course. Oh, everything is working out! I never dreamed I'd keep my house and have young people stay with me, too!"

"I'm happy for you, Althea," Grandfather said. "But it's time we Aldens headed back home."

"I don't know how I can ever repay you," Althea said.

"We don't need any payment," Henry said, speaking for all the Aldens. "We had fun finding the treasure."

David stepped forward, his hands behind his back. "I have something Benny might want," he said.

He presented Benny with a peacock feather. It was a glorious reward, almost as tall as Benny, with a sapphire eye on the end.

"Oh, boy!" Benny exclaimed. "Thanks a lot, David!"

Outside, the peacock gave his eerie cry.

"He doesn't want this back, does he?" Benny asked. "Can peacocks count their tail feathers?"

Everyone laughed.

"No, Benny," Jessie said. "I don't think birds can count as well as you can!"

She was glad they had found the secret of Peacock Hall and saved the wonderful old house.

And they could count on another mystery just around the corner!

GERTRUDE CHANDLER WARNER discovered when she was teaching that many readers who like an exciting story could find no books that were both easy and fun to read. She decided to try to meet this need, and her first book, *The Boxcar Children*, quickly proved she had succeeded.

Miss Warner drew on her own experiences to write the mystery. As a child she spent hours watching trains go by on the tracks opposite her family home. She often dreamed about what it would be like to set up housekeeping in a caboose or freight car—the situation the Alden children find themselves in.

While the mystery element is central to each of Miss Warner's books, she never thought of them as strictly juvenile mysteries. She liked to stress the Aldens' independence and resourcefulness and their solid New England devotion to using up and making do. The Aldens go about most of their adventures with as little adult supervision as possible—something else that delights young readers.

Miss Warner lived in Putnam, Connecticut, until her death in 1979. During her lifetime, she received hundreds of letters from girls and boys telling her how much they liked her books.